THE POWER OF THE FORTREX

Written by Rebecca L. Schmidt

SCHOLASTIC

Scholastic Children's Books,
Euston House,
24 Eversholt Street,
London NW1 1DB, UK

A division of Scholastic Ltd
London ~ New York ~ Toronto ~ Sydney ~ Auckland
Mexico City ~ New Delhi ~ Hong Kong

This book was first published in the US in 2016 by Scholastic Inc.
Published in the UK by Scholastic Ltd, 2016

ISBN 978 1407 16273 7

Printed in Italy

2 4 6 8 10 9 7 5 3 1

Papers used by Scholastic Children's Books are made from
woods grown in sustainable forests.

www.scholastic.co.uk

MIX
Paper from
responsible sources
FSC® C023419

Knight Fight!

"**F**orm up on me! The Lord Nordby Defence! Nordby, Nordby, Nordby!" Clay ordered. He and the NEXO KNIGHTS team were defending a small town from a mob of Jestro's evil Magma Monsters. But the knights were having trouble – a lot of trouble.

Macy was too busy fighting to hear Clay's instructions. There were Magma Monsters everywhere! What the knights needed now were their NEXO Powers. Macy knew if they could just connect to Merlok 2.0's Operating System, they would have all the armour and weapons they needed. But her NEXO Shield had no signal! The knights would have to win this battle without Merlok 2.0's help.

Meanwhile, all the knights were having trouble working together. But Lance and Clay were the worst. They even started to attack each other by mistake!

"Whose side are you even on?" Lance asked Clay angrily.

Before they knew it, all the knights had been knocked to the ground. The Magma Monsters had won! What were the knights going to do?

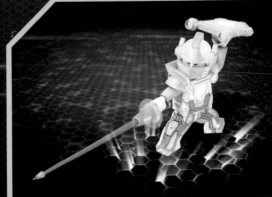

Merlok Glitches

Suddenly, the Magma Monsters and the small town burst into digital pieces.

"Terrible! Just terrible!" Merlok 2.0 said. Squirebots carried the digi-wizard into the Holo-Training Gym, where the knights had been practising. They were lucky it hadn't been a real battle! "There is an ancient, mystical phrase you've obviously never heard of called 'team-

Clay knew exactly who to blame for the knights' failure. "It's your fault we keep losing, Lance," Clay said. "The key to teamwork, is, uh, *working together*!"

But Lance wasn't interested in Clay's ideas. "Until you accept that I'm in charge, I can't work with you," he said.

Merlok 2.0 watched the two knights fighting. Enough was enough!

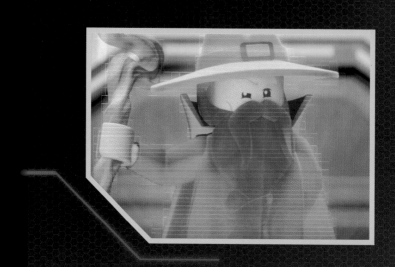

"It is not who is in charge, or who downloads the biggest weapon. It's about working as a team," the wizard said. But as Merlok 2.0 spoke, his voice kept fading in and out. The knights could barely understand him.

Ava, the team's tech genius, told the knights there wasn't enough power to keep Merlok 2.0's program running.

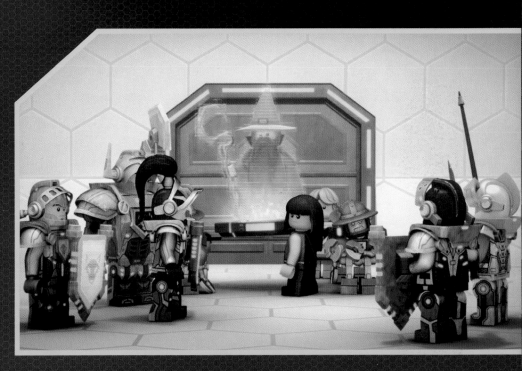

That's why Macy hadn't been able to download her NEXO Power: the wizard's signal wasn't strong enough. Without Merlok 2.0 in working order, Macy and the other knights would never be able to defeat Jestro and his Magma Monsters. Ava and her fellow knight-in-training, Robin, promised to try and fix Merlok 2.0 as quickly as possible.

There's No "I" in Team

The knights were tired after a long day of training. All they wanted to do was relax. But Clay had other ideas. He flipped through the battle manual he had prepared for everyone.

"OK. We made some real progress today, knights. I'm glad everyone agreed to learn my offensive and defensive set plays, because I really think they've got a lot to offer," Clay said proudly.

Aaron snorted. Macy sighed. Axl was hungry.
"Look, Captain Knight-tastic," Lance said, "wh[...]
we need now is to relax. And definitely for you t[...]
stop talking."

Clay was upset. Lance hadn't even read his battle manual!

Macy groaned. Would Clay and Lance ever get along? "Should we do something?" she asked, looking at the bickering knights.

"Too tired and not care-y," Aaron said.

Before Clay and Lance's argument could break into an all-out fight, a Squirebot ran up to them. While the knights had been arguing, Jestro and The Book of Monsters had destroyed the Hamlet of Omelette!

"They had such good omelettes," Axl sighed, rubbing his empty stomach.

The NEXO KNIGHTS team needed to protect the realm – even without their NEXO Powers. But there was another problem: Omelette was on the other side of the kingdom! The knights had no way to *get* to the monsters.

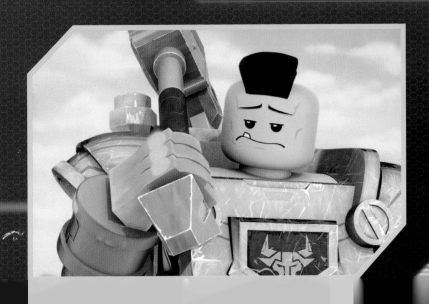

A Mighty Fortrex

Just then, the king and queen rode up in a giant rolling castle. They had come back from their royal duties as soon as they heard about the monsters' attacks.

"Ah! I totally forgot about Ye Olde Royal caravan. Dad, do you know what we could do with this?" Macy asked the king, looking up at the large castle on wheels.

"Journey the countryside in peaceful comfort?" the king replied, confused.

But the knights had other plans. They would change the royal caravan into a rolling fortress called the Fortrex. That way, Merlok 2.0's program could travel everywhere with the NEXO KNIGHTS team. Plus, the towers would boost the signal for their NEXO Powers! This could solve all their problems!

The next morning, Ava and Robin gave the
NEXO KNIGHTS team a tour of the Fortrex. They
had upgraded it with a full armoury, a Holo-deck
training area, a kitchen, and bedrooms! There
were even video games for downtime.

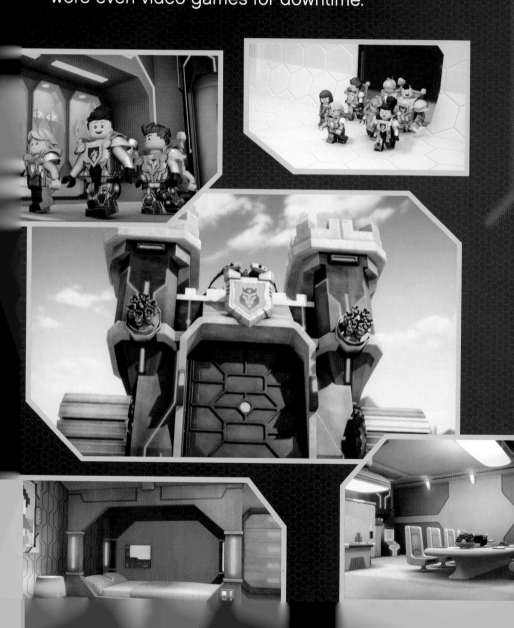

Merlok 2.0 was in the control room, but Ava hadn't figured out how to transfer him into the Fortrex's systems yet. Until she did, the knights wouldn't be able to download their powers.

Clay wasn't worried. "You'll get it, Ava. The good news is, we're taking the fight to Jestro."

Parting Gifts

The king and queen had one more present for the knights before they left. A slick, new car sped up and stopped right in front of Clay. It was called the Rumble Blade. Now the knights would be able to zoom right into the action.

"Now, that is a fine-looking piece of machinery," Clay said. It would be perfect for him, Macy and Axl.

Aaron would never need a car when he had his hover shield. And Lance had his transport covered, too. A mecha-steed ran up and neighed right next to Clay's new car.

"Uh, isn't a mecha-steed a little 'old-fashioned'?" Macy asked.

But Lance had a few tricks up his sleeve. The mecha-steed transformed into his own personal car – complete with a golden lance!

Jestro Attacks!

The knights were ready – and just in time!
Merlok 2.0 told the knights Jestro was attacking
Waterton. If the knights didn't stop him, a third of
the kingdom would be without water.

Lance was especially worried: no water meant no Jacuzzis! "There's no time to waste, man!" Lance told Clay. "We need that teamwork thing you've been talking about! Let's go!"

Clay smiled. Lance wasn't going to change his ways overnight, but this was a start.

Now that they had the Fortrex and their new cars, nothing could stand in the knights' way. Having Lance fight as part of the team wouldn't hurt, either!

The knights sped off to Waterton. They just hoped they wouldn't be too late.

The Battle of Waterton

In Waterton, villagers screamed in panic as Magma Monsters attacked the town. Jestro and his evil partner, The Book of Monsters, laughed. Nothing could stop them!

Suddenly, they heard a loud roar. Jestro couldn't believe it – was that the king's old caravan?

The knights burst out of the Fortrex with the new vehicles. Jestro and The Book of Monst were shocked.

"They have cars?" Jestro whined.

"Time for a pincer attack!" Clay ordered. With the press of a button, Macy's and Axl's seats ejected from the car, giving them their own Knight Cycles! The Magma Monsters were surrounded.

But the knights' NEXO Powers still weren't working.

"We could use the Whirling Macy to break up that monster pack," Lance suggested.

Clay couldn't believe it. Lance had read his battle manual after all! Together, the two knights charged towards the incoming army of Magma Monsters. They just hoped that Ava was making progress with Merlok 2.0.

Techcalibur

nside the Fortrex, Ava knew that the knights couldn't defeat the monsters without their NEXO Powers. It was time for desperate measures. She told Merlok 2.0 about Techcalibur, a flash drive that could transfer Merlok 2.0 into the Fortrex's main systems. The only problem was she hadn't tested it yet. If it didn't work, Merlok 2.0 could be lost forever.

Merlok 2.0 told Ava that they didn't have a choice. "I know you can work your magic, too. Now make it so!" Merlok 2.0 said.

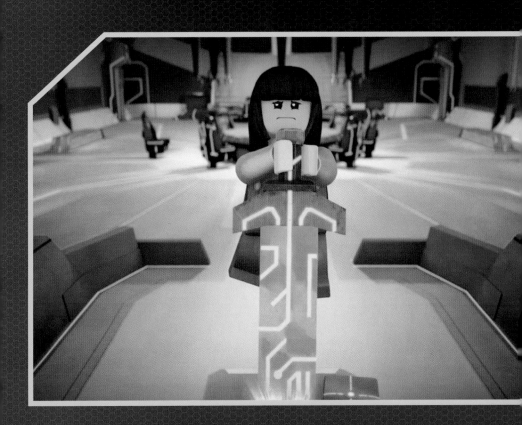

Ava transferred Merlok 2.0 into Techcalibur. The wizard's hologram disappeared. Then, Ava ran over to the Fortrex's main computer and uploaded Merlok 2.0's program. She hurried back to the pedestal – had it worked?

"Yes! Get ready for NEXO Scan!" Merlok 2.0 said as his hologram reappeared. Ava had saved Merlok 2.0 – and the knights!

Back on the battlefield, the knights were fighting as hard as they could. But they didn't know how much longer they could last.

Just then, Macy saw her shield light up! They could finally download their NEXO Powers!

Teamwork!

The five knights held up their shields. "NEXOOOO Knight!" Macy cheered.

"NEXO Power: Alliance of the Fortrex!" Merlok 2.0 announced as he sent the download to the knights. Suddenly, their armours and weapons lit up. Now, the knights had all the power they needed to defeat Jestro, The Book of Monsters, and their Magma Monsters!

Lance's mecha-steed roared after Burnzie as Macy beat back Globlins with her mace. Clay slid under Sparkks' legs and knocked him down from behind. There was no way that the Magma Monsters would get away this time. After each attack, the monsters disappeared in puffs of purple smoke.

Working as a team, the NEXO KNIGHTS heroes soon defeated the monsters.

The Book of Monsters and Jestro knew they had been beaten. It was time to make a run for it!

The team smiled as they watched the evil duo retreat.

"Uh, Clay. Do we have to pose heroically after every battle?" Macy asked.

"Yes. It's in the battle manual. 'Approved Post-Battle Celebrations' section," Clay said.

Later that day, Clay, Lance and the other knights celebrated their victory in the Fortrex.

"A toast!" Clay said, raising his class.

"The united knights!" everyone said in unison.

Clay smiled at his teammates. He knew that the knights would be able to face whatever Jestro was planning. Together.